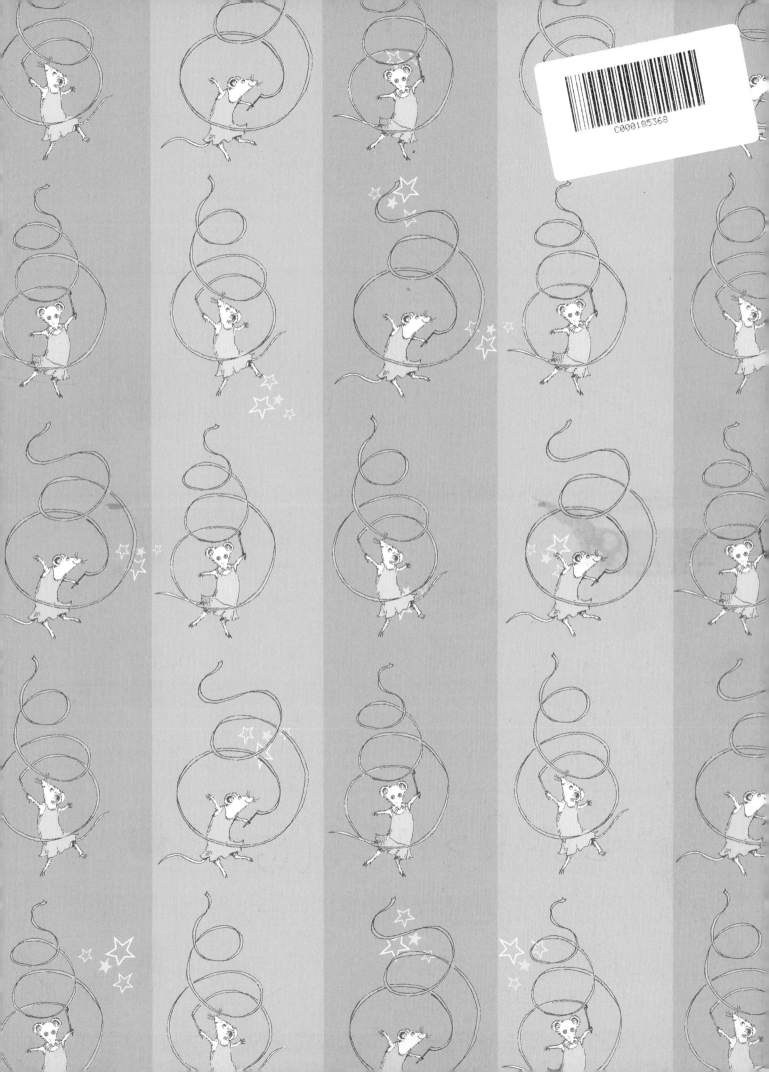

This Angelina Ballerina Annual belongs to

Lucy Remedios

Annual 2009

Contents

EGMONT

We bring stories to life

First published in Great Britain 2008 by Egmont UK Limited
239 Kensington High Street, London W8 6SA
Angelina Ballerina © 2008 Helen Craig Ltd. and Katharine Holabird. The Angelina Ballerina
name and character and the dancing Angelina logo are trademarks of HIT Entertainment
Limited, Katharine Holabird and Helen Craig. Reg. U.S. Pat. & Tm. Off.
Stories adapted from original scripts by Andrew Brenner, Paul Larson, Jan Page,
Diane Redmond and Barbara Slade.
All rights reserved.
ISBN 978 1 4052 3910 3
1 3 5 7 9 10 8 6 4 2
Printed in Italy

HiT entertainment

Angelina Ballerina ™

Hello, it's so lovely to meet you!
Do you dream of becoming a star
ballerina, just like I do?
I know that with lots of hard work
i'll get there one day!
Love,
Angelina x

I'm sure you all know me, Angelina, but let me introduce some of my family and friends in Mouseland – that's where I live, in a village called Chipping Cheddar.

Mrs Mouseling

First meet my mum, Matilda Mouseling. She looks after us all – here she is, brushing my younger sister Polly's tummy. She cooks the best cheese pies and makes my beautiful ballet costumes.

Mr Mouseling

Here's my dad, Maurice Mouseling, playing the fiddle. He loves music, telling jokes, having fun and eating. But he also works really hard running the Mouseland Gazette newspaper.

My Friends!

♡♡♡ Polly ♡♡♡

Isn't my little sister, Polly, cute? She's only tiny, but we still have lots of fun together playing little games. Sometimes, I try and teach her to dance, but she's still so small!

♡♡♡ Grandma ♡♡♡ and Grandpa

I do love it when my grandma and grandpa come to visit from the next village. They like to hear all about what I've been up to and I love to hear their stories about the past, too!

♡♡♡ Alice ♡♡♡

This is my very best friend, Alice Nimbletoes. She's really good at gymnastics – look at her doing a cartwheel! We always have lots of fun together because Alice loves adventures and I love sharing them with her.

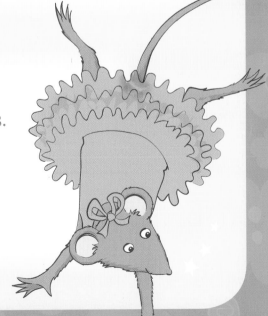

Henry

Have you got any cousins? Henry's my cousin and because he's a little bit younger than me, I sometimes have to look after him. But we still enjoy spending time together and some days he even comes to ballet class.

Miss Lilly

You really must meet my ballet teacher, Miss Lilly. Did you know she used to be a star ballerina herself? She comes from a far-off country called Dacovia, but I'm glad she came to Chipping Cheddar to open her wonderful ballet school.

♥♥♥ William ♥♥♥

Alice told me that my friend William thinks I'm the best thing since sliced cheese, but I don't know if that's true – do you? William comes to Miss Lilly's ballet classes, but I don't think he really wants to be a ballet star like me.

♥♥♥ Priscilla and Penelope Pinkpaws ♥♥♥

I'd better warn you about the Pinkpaws twins because they are not always very nice to me, especially when we're all at Miss Lilly's ballet class. Sometimes they say unfriendly things or laugh at me and I don't like that at all!

The Rose Fairy

Miss Lilly was choosing a dancer to be the Rose Fairy Princess. "You'll be the best Rose Fairy Princess in all of Mouseland, Angelina," said Alice.

But as she danced, Angelina tripped over her untied ribbon. "I'd make a better Princess," boasted Penelope Pinkpaws to her twin sister, Priscilla.

But Miss Lilly did choose Angelina as her Princess. "And you, Penelope, like Alice, will be a beautiful dancing flower," she added.

Angelina was delighted! "I'm going to practise every day, ten times a day," she told Alice and William. "I'm going to be the best Rose Fairy Princess ever!"

Princess

But as she was leaving class, Angelina heard Miss Lilly explaining, "… and Angelina will fly across the stage on a single wire – it will be marvellous!"

Now Angelina was worried! "A single wire!" she repeated to herself, not liking the sound of it at all. It was no good, she had to talk to Miss Lilly!

But Miss Lilly wouldn't change her mind. "You will soar above the stage like a bird, my dear Angelina," she said. "You will be magnificent!"

Angelina needed a plan! "Come on, Alice," she said, "we've got to find Zivo, the famous trapeze artist. I think he might be able to help me."

Soon the two mouselings arrived at the Big Top, where Zivo performed his daring act. "I'm sure Zivo can help me fly," said Angelina, nervously.

They found Zivo on the high trapeze. "Of course I can help, Angelina," he said. Soon, Angelina was swinging through the air on the trapeze, too.

Angelina climbed bravely to the high platform. But as she looked up, she spotted the hook that would attach her harness to the wire and disaster struck!

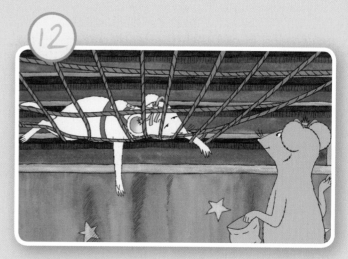

Angelina fainted and fell through the air – luckily she landed on the bouncy safety net. But now she was more scared of flying than ever!

It didn't get much better at rehearsals. At first Angelina was fine, practising her Rose Fairy Princess dances with the dancing flowers around her.

But then Miss Lilly called out, "Are you ready for the finale? Angelina, come fly!" And with that, Angelina fainted right there on the stage.

"Oh dear, I suspect our Angelina is afraid," whispered Penelope naughtily. "I could always be the Princess, Miss Lilly," she offered.

But Miss Lilly would hear none of it. "No more flying today," she declared. "Angelina, my darlink, go home and rest your paws."

Soon it was the day of the show! "I bought you a present, for luck," said Alice. "Not that you'll need it." Angelina wasn't so sure!

Inside the theatre, Angelina suddenly had an idea. "Why don't you fly instead, Alice? We could swap just before the finale, no one would know."

By the time the show started, the plan was in place. Angelina was a perfect Rose Fairy Princess and Alice a delightful dancing flower.

Just before the finale, Angelina danced off stage to where the flying harness was stored. She beckoned Alice over to change costumes, as planned.

"My costume's got caught!" whispered Alice, trying to free it. "The show must go on," thought Angelina, as she pulled on her harness.

Angelina was soon flying triumphantly across the stage. "I couldn't let Miss Lilly down," she thought, "and after all, I am the Rose Fairy Princess!"

Back at Cheddar Cottage, Angelina was telling Alice about her idea for Miss Lilly's next show. "It can be a ballet about the circus," she said.

"Of course, I will play a dancing circus girl, who flies across the stage on a single wire," added Angelina. "It will be the best ballet ever!"

six to spot!

Angelina really loves being the Rose Fairy Princess!
These pictures of the show look the same. Can you
spot 6 differences in picture 2?

say the Word

Alice has written a poem about being a Dancing Flower. Which of these 3 words fits in each space to make it rhyme?

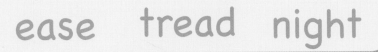

ease   tread   night

Flower garland above my head,

On the stage I softly 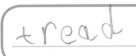 tread .

Dancing on my toes so light,

On this very special  night .

A Dancing Flower in the breeze,

Swaying with the greatest 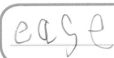 ease .

Welcome to Winter ... with Alice

Angelina and I just love to go ice skating when Miller's Pond freezes over!

One of these pictures of Angelina is different from the rest. Can you spot the odd one out?

Poor Henry has fallen on the slippery ice! Which ice skate trail should I take to help him get up again?

a   f   c

21

Angelina -

It was the last day of the summer term at Miss Lilly's Ballet School.

"My darlinks, have a glorious holiday and I will see you all in a few weeks for the start of the new term," said Miss Lilly, as she waved the class goodbye.

Soon, Alice and William were talking excitedly about a summer of sandcastles, seashells – and ice cream!

"Won't it be wonderful, Angelina?" said William, but Angelina shook her head, as the Pinkpaws twins chipped in.

"Oh, we forgot, you're not going on holiday, are you,

22

Ace Reporter!

Angelina?" the twins sniggered. Alice gently led Angelina out of the room.

"There are lots of fun things to do in Chipping Cheddar, Angelina," said Alice.

"You can play with Henry," said William, spotting Angelina's cousin taking pictures with his camera.

"There's no way I'm spending my whole summer holiday playing with Henry," said Angelina sulkily.

Back at Cheddar Cottage, Henry asked Angelina if she wanted to help him take photos of flowers with his camera.

"No!" snapped Angelina, and with that, she turned to Mrs Mouseling, complaining, "I'm the only mouseling not going on holiday!"

"I'm sorry, Angelina," said Mrs Mouseling, "but the opera starts next week and your father has to interview the star, Maria Mozzarella, for a special edition of the Mouseland Gazette."

Just then, Mr Mouseling came into the kitchen.

"I don't believe it!" he moaned, "Maria Mozzarella now says she doesn't do interviews. I'm going to have to find someone else to interview today, or there won't be a special edition of the Gazette at all – I'm afraid it's going to be a very long day!"

"It's going to be a very long two weeks," muttered Angelina to herself.

Mr Mouseling rushed out of the house, leaving his lunchbox behind.

"It's OK," said Angelina to

Mrs Mouseling, "I'll take it to his office."

"Thank you, Angelina," said Mr Mouseling, as she handed over the lunchbox. "But I don't think I'll have time to eat lunch. I've got to go and interview another singer from the opera – Cameron Cheesecloth.

Today is such a busy day!"

But before Mr Mouseling could leave for his interview, the phone rang. It was Mr Inkspot, the Mouseland Gazette's printer, ringing to say he was too ill to come into work.

"Could I help with the special edition, Dad?" asked Angelina. "I haven't got anything else to do and I've seen Mr Inkspot work the press a hundred times."

Mr Mouseling wasn't sure it was

a good idea, but he didn't have time to look after the printer and do the interview, so he agreed.

"I won't let you down, Dad," said Angelina, as she got to work.

But things soon went from bad to worse! First, Angelina turned on the office fan, accidentally

blowing the printing paper all around the room. Then she collected a bottle of the ink off the shelf. But when Angelina tried to take the stopper out of the bottle, it was stuck. As she struggled, the stopper suddenly flew out and the ink spilled everywhere – including all over Angelina and Mr Mouseling!

"I really must remember what Mr Inkspot does," thought Angelina, as she turned to the printing press. She switched it on and was amazed to find it

worked! Even Mr Mouseling was surprised.

"It's a very complicated machine, and can easily break down," he said.

Just then, it shuddered to a halt. Mr Mouseling was sure to miss the interview now, as he would have to stay and fix it.

Angelina felt rather bad. "Perhaps I could do the interview for you?" she offered. Mr Mouseling wasn't sure she would be confident enough to interview someone as famous as Cameron Cheesecloth.

It took some persuasion, but Mr Mouseling finally agreed. "You'd better run along, Angelina," he said. "You don't want to keep Mr Cheesecloth waiting." So off she hurried.

How will the interview go? Turn to page 42 to find out!

say cheese!

Henry loves to take pictures with his camera! Here are some photographs from his album but can you fill in the missing word to describe what's happening in each one?

1

cake

hug

wave

Alice gave Angelina a big _____.

2

bed

swing

bicycle

Poor Angelina fell off her _____.

3

football

tennis

cards

The game of [_____] was very exciting!

4

cars

houses

seats

The audience waited in their [_____].

5

green

purple

orange

William wore a [_____] party hat.

29

step into spring ...
with Miss Lilly

My darlink Angelina is helping me with some spring cleaning. Can you circle 8 different things that start with the letter b?

Answer: bucket, brush, bow, ballet shoe, buttons, box, books, bracelets.

My beautiful ballerinas are doing a spring dance and their dress colours make such a pretty pattern! Can you colour in the dresses (and the flowers) to complete the pattern.

Start

Finish

Answer: the pattern of the dress colours is pink, blue, yellow, so the sixth ballerina's dress is yellow, the eighth is blue, the tenth is pink and the eleventh is blue to complete the pattern.

Lights, Camera,

Angelina and her friends were at the cinema. "Oh, I'd love to be a movie star," whispered Angelina, "and see my name up in lights!"

On the way out, Alice spotted a big poster for a film-making competition. "Perfect!" cried Angelina. "Let's make a film and enter."

"I'd love to be in a film too," said Alice, but Angelina was already too lost in her own dreams of being a star to listen.

Angelina had her own ideas for a film. "I'll star as the mouseling who breaks her tail but triumphs as a dancer. We're bound to win the competition!"

Action!

There was only one problem – they didn't have a film camera. Henry was sure that Dr Tuttle had one, if he would just let them use it.

So off they went to see Dr Tuttle, who pulled a big book from his shelf. "The story of Thomasina Tuttle, the perfect plot," he said.

"And there's a great role for a brave doctor who saves Thomasina's life," he added. "That's the story we shall film!" cried Angelina.

Once the mouselings had agreed to give Dr Tuttle the role of the brave doctor, he handed them his camera and they left to read the book.

After reading the book, Angelina was not happy. "Thomasina's a farm girl, she doesn't wear a tutu. And I'm not falling in a hole like she did," she said.

Soon, Angelina was busy handing out jobs. "William on camera, Alice can get props and Henry, you can be my assistant!"

"And what will I be doing in the role of the clever best friend?" asked Alice. "We're not having that role," said Angelina, crossly.

They began to film. "It's just all black," said William, looking through the camera lens. "That's because the cap's still on!" snapped Angelina.

Angelina's temper didn't get any better. "Must I do everything?" she shouted. "It's not easy being the movie star *and* the director."

With that, Alice and William decided they had had enough and scampered off, leaving poor Henry to take over filming Angelina's starring role.

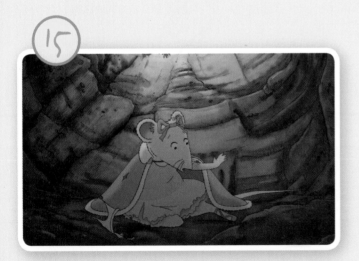

Alice and William hadn't got very far before they heard a loud scream – Angelina had fallen down a hole and she was stuck!

Alice rushed back. "We'll get you out, Angelina," she called. She tied a rope to a tree stump and William climbed down the rope, into the hole.

17

"This is just like the real story of
Thomasina Tuttle," said Henry,
grabbing the camera and pointing
it down into the hole.

18

Just then, the rope broke loose and
sent William tumbling into the hole
with Angelina! How sorry she was
for shouting at her friends now.

19

William threw the rope back up and
soon Alice had tied it more tightly.
William was able to help Angelina
climb out of the hole.

20

Angelina was very relieved after their
escape. "You're so brave, William,"
she said, making him blush. "And I
really am sorry for shouting at you."

Just then, Dr Tuttle arrived. He started acting straightaway, until Alice said, "I'm afraid Angelina's hurt her paw. You'll have to look at that first."

All the time, Henry kept filming so they still had a film to enter in the competition. At the film festival they were delighted to find they had won!

"The Story of Thomasina Tuttle is one of the funniest films I've ever seen," laughed the Chair of Judges, after they had shown the film.

"I dedicate the prize to my cousin, Henry," added Angelina, handing the trophy to him. "This trophy belongs to you for filming everything!"

Tell the story!

Can you remember what happened in the 'Lights, Camera, Action!' story? Write the correct order for the pictures and captions in the empty boxes. No peeking at the story!

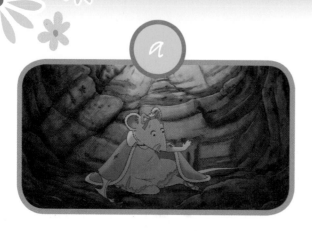

Angelina falls down the hole and gets stuck!

Angelina and Alice go to see a film.

Angelina dedicates the prize to Henry.

William tumbles into the hole with Angelina!

Write your answers in the boxes.

① ② ③ ④ ⑤ ⑥ ⑦ ⑧

Dr Tuttle lends Alice and Angelina a camera.

Angelina tells Alice there's no role for her.

Alice and William have had enough and leave.

Angelina hands out jobs to everyone.

A sunny summer ... with Henry

Here are some poems about the things I like doing in the summer holidays. Write the letter of the poem next to the matching picture of me.

a

All my toys are lots of fun.
The blue train is my
favourite one!

1

2

b

If I hear a lively song,
I'll dance and dance
the whole day long!

c I love to bake a tasty treat, especially one I get to eat!

3

d My lovely cousin spins me round, 'til my feet lift off the ground!

4

e Dressing up is fun, you see, being what you want to be.

5

How many of Henry's toy trains can you see hidden around the page?

I need to have the right hat," she thought, looking at the perfect reporter's hat in the window.

Just then, Henry appeared with his camera and asked Angelina if she wanted to take some photos of flowers or stones. When she explained about the interview, Henry asked if he could come along, too.

"Only if you promise to tell me when the bus comes," agreed Angelina. And with

Angelina was hurrying through Chipping Cheddar on her way to her interview with opera star, Cameron Cheesecloth, when she passed a hat shop.

"If I'm going to be a reporter,

Henry looking out, she went into the shop to buy her hat.

But just as Angelina came out again wearing her new hat, the bus whizzed past. They had missed it!

Henry and Angelina had to run all the way to the theatre. Angelina was quite breathless as she explained to the doorman that she had come to interview Cameron Cheesecloth.

"You've just missed him," said the doorman.

"Oh no!" she cried. "Which way did he go?"

"Try the stage door," said the doorman. "You might just catch him."

Angelina raced to the stage door, just in time to see the back of Cameron Cheesecloth's

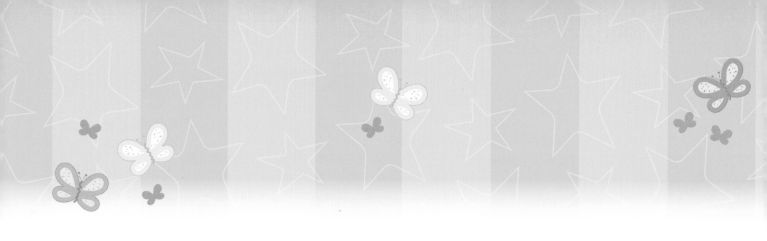

car as he drove away. She was too late to get her interview!

Back in Mrs Thimble's shop, Angelina and Henry bought ice creams to cheer themselves up. "This will be the first time there hasn't been a special edition of the Mouseland Gazette," wailed Angelina, "and it's all my fault!" "Perhaps everyone will have forgotten about it?" suggested Henry, licking his ice cream.

But no such luck. As Mrs Thimble handed Angelina her ice cream she said, "Tell your father we're all really looking forward to the special edition." It seemed no one had forgotten, after all.

As Angelina and Henry left the shop with their ice creams, they were too busy eating and talking to notice the smartly dressed chauffeur changing the

wheel on a rather grand car.

"It's all Maria Mozzarella's fault," Angelina was saying to Henry. "Fancy being too famous to give interviews – I mean, without her fans, she wouldn't even be famous. When I'm a famous ballerina, I'll give lots of interviews. After all, stars have a duty to their fans, don't you think?"

Just then, an elegant mouse stepped out

of the grand-looking car and turned to Angelina.

"You are so right, my dear little mousling. I, Maria Mozzarella, should be ashamed of myself."

Angelina and Henry couldn't believe their ears!

Back at the office, Mr Mouseling had fixed the printing machine. When Angelina came back, she told him she'd missed Cameron Cheesecloth. Mr Mouseling pretended not to be disappointed, but he couldn't fool Angelina. She quickly told him all about Maria Mozzarella.

Later that day, Mr Mouseling couldn't believe his eyes, as he held up the front page of his special edition. There, in black and white, was a photograph of Maria Mozzarella, alongside Angelina's interview with the opera star.

"This is much better than Cameron Cheesecloth,

Angelina," said Mr Mouseling. "You really have done a marvellous job. I just can't understand how you managed to get a photograph and an interview with Miss Mozzarella – it's the perfect front page for the special edition."

"Well, if Miss Mozzarella's car hadn't had a puncture and Henry hadn't had his camera, I couldn't have done it," explained Angelina.

"Ah, but you seized your opportunity, Angelina," said Mr Mouseling. "And that is what makes an ace reporter."

Angelina was so proud.

"Thanks, Dad," she said. "And you know what, when I'm a famous ballerina, I'll let you interview me any time you like," she offered.

"You'd better!" answered Mr Mouseling, and they both laughed happily as Angelina danced around the office.

Who's in the News?

Chipping Cheddar

MOUSELAND GAZETTE

Monday 5th January 2009

ANGELINA – BALLERINA AND STAR REPORTER!

Friends of Angelina Mouseling already know what a talented dancer she is, but they might be surprised to find out she is an excellent journalist, too. Yesterday, long after other reporters would have given up the chase, Angelina managed to get an interview with famous opera star, Maria Mozzarella.

POLLY LOVES HER PRETTY NEW DRESS

Little Polly Mouseling got a brand-new, pretty pink dress yesterday. Polly loves it so much that she wants to wear it every day, leaving Mrs Mouseling no time to wash it.

HAPPY BIRTHDAY TO HENRY!

Henry Mouseling celebrates his birthday today. Henry likes taking photographs, his blue toy train and his cousin, Angelina. We hope you get lots of presents, Henry!

Angelina and Alice have made their own special edition of the Mouseland Gazette. Draw the pictures that go with each story in the white boxes.

A GREAT DAY OUT WITH GRANDMA MOUSELING

Angelina and her best friend, Alice, had a great day out with Grandma Mouseling. Angelina's grandma was visiting Chipping Cheddar from the next village and took the two ballerinas out for afternoon tea. Then they went to see a film about the ballet. Alice said it was "a great day out" and Angelina agreed.

WILLIAM AND SAMMY FIND SOME TREASURE!

William and Sammy joined forces to have an amazing adventure. The mismatched mice paired up to find the legendary lost treasure of Chipping Cheddar. After searching for clues all afternoon, the two friends were tired and hungry. They were just about to go home when Sammy stubbed his toe on a heavy wooden box. Could it be the lost treasure?

All About Autumn ... with

I watched Angelina practise her ballet steps in front of a mirror before the Chipping Cheddar autumn show. Can you spot 6 differences between Angelina in the studio and the reflection in the mirror?

50

Mr and Mrs Mouseling

The autumn show was a triumph! Angelina and
I entertained the crowds with music and dancing.
Colour in the picture to make it look bright
and cheerful – just like the show!

Angelina and Alice were in the village shop buying cheesy treats, when Angelina spotted a leaflet announcing a competition for Teacher of the Year.

"Alice, no one deserves this award more than Miss Lilly," she cried. "We must enter her. She's sure to win!" So they hurried home to write a letter.

Back at Cheddar Cottage, Angelina and Alice wrote a long list of all the reasons why Miss Lilly was the best teacher in all of Mouseland.

The next day in ballet class, Angelina asked Penelope and Priscilla Pinkpaws to sign the letter, telling them all about the competition.

"Sign this!" she whispered to William, who, as Prince Charming, was supposed to be kissing Angelina's Sleeping Beauty to wake her up.

"What is going on?" demanded Miss Lilly. "Concentrate, class. We must practise very hard to be ready for our summer show."

Once everyone had signed the letter, Angelina and Alice took it to the postbox. "Squash it in," said Alice. "Today's the last day to enter!"

A few days later, the mouselings were still rehearsing when the postman arrived with a very grand-looking letter for Miss Lilly.

"Letters for later!" cried Miss Lilly, as she put it down. "But Miss Lilly," said Angelina, "It looks awfully important. Perhaps you should open it now?"

So Miss Lilly opened the letter and discovered that she had won the Best Teacher Award! "I never expected anything like this!" she cried, happily.

Of course the news had to be reported in the Mouseland Gazette and, later that day, Mr Mouseling took a photo of Miss Lilly and Angelina.

But when Angelina showed the paper to her friends, the Pinkpaws twins just laughed when they saw that Angelina had been almost cut out of the shot.

At class, things got worse when Miss Quaver announced that Miss Lilly was at a gala dinner and so she would be taking rehearsals instead.

Although she tried her hardest, Miss Quaver was no ballet teacher and the mouselings seemed to be dancing all over the place!

When Miss Lilly returned to class, she was so tired from travelling and attending award parties, that she fell asleep during practice!

"This is no good," cried Angelina, banging down the piano lid as she tried to wake her sleeping teacher. "We need to practise!"

After class, Angelina and Alice were in the shop buying ice cream when they saw Miss Lilly and Miss Quaver walking past.

"... and so," they heard Miss Lilly say, "I will have to give it up. I just can't find the time to teach my dance classes, Miss Quaver."

"Miss Lilly, give up teaching?" cried Angelina. "I wish we'd never entered her for this stupid competition in the first place!"

The next day, Angelina was quick to speak to Miss Lilly, "You can't give up teaching, we need you! It's just a silly award anyway!"

"Oh, my darlink Angelina," replied Miss Lilly, softly. "I could never give up teaching my mouselings. It is the award I shall give up."

And so Miss Lilly and Angelina attended the prize-giving ceremony, where Angelina was first to take the microphone.

"My ballet teacher, Miss Lilly, isn't just the best teacher in Mouseland," she said in a shaky voice. "She's the best teacher in the whole world!"

And the headline in the next day's Mouseland Gazette told the story: 'Teacher Chooses Mouselings Over Prestigious Award!'

Mrs Thimble's Missing Pieces

1 b

2

3 g

4 a